*ADRIAN TOWNSEND*

# Grandad's Gang

*Illustrated by Kate Chesterton*

First Published 2011 By
Grassy Hill Publishing
52 Wheatley Road Garsington Oxford OX44 9ER

Text Copyright © 2011 Adrian Townsend
Illustrations Copyright © 2011 Kate Chesterton

ISBN 978-1-903569-10-9

# Grandad's Gang

To my best mate

Donnie Campbell

# Contents

# Grandad's Gang

My grandad's got a gang. There are four people in it and they're trouble. At least that's what my dad says. He says they should grow up and stop messing about. But that's what I like about them. They're really cool and they do some fantastic things. They're always up to something, "mostly no good," says my dad, but he doesn't understand how brilliant they are. I call my grandad 'Gramps' and he meets up with his gang every Friday night in the Jolly Farmer pub in our village. That's when they "get up to things," as my dad calls it. They plan their latest projects as they play dominoes and drink beer. My dad won't go into the Jolly Farmer on Fridays. He says he doesn't want to be embarrassed by them. He also says he's never met a jolly farmer.

Gramps and his gang have all known each other for a long time. They all met at primary school and dad says they've never really grown up. I think my dad's a bit jealous because his mates are all very sensible. He's probably a bit fed up too, because Gramps' gang tend to play quite a few jokes on him, like the time they planted fake plants in his garden. Dad thought he had grown some really special plants before he saw the gang hiding and laughing behind the hedge and he noticed that all the plants were plastic and from the local supermarket. Anyway, I'll tell you some more of the things they get up to but first I had better tell you who they are. My grandad's real name is Kenneth but everybody calls him Ken. The others are called Morris, Trevor and Winston. Winston is the youngest member of the gang and he still works part time. He could have retired years ago. He's a scientist and does lots of experiments, and he's so brainy the laboratory where he works have asked him to carry on working two days a week.

Winston was born in Tobago, which is hot and sunny in the Caribbean. Winston hates cold, wet weather even though he should be used to it by now. He came to our village with his mum and dad when he was two years old. Winston's dad worked in the car factory near to our village. Winston's dad made him work hard at school and he went to Oxford University before he became a scientist.

The best bit about Winston is the way he works things out. He makes plans and designs things even without a computer. He says things like "in theory the answer has two possible solutions..." and "what we really need to do is..." Everybody knows that his brain is working really hard when he pulls a pencil from his pocket and starts scribbling on a piece of paper. Winston is the brains behind most of Gramps' gangs 'projects' but he is not very good with his hands.

When the gang need to make things they turn to Trevor. Trevor used to work in the car factory too, and he can make anything work. He is brilliant at building things. He's got his own vintage car called an Austin Seven. He built and repaired it from a heap of old parts. He's so practical he can fix anything that's broken. I like Trevor because he takes me to football training. He used to play semi-professional football before he got injured and went to work in the factory. My dad quite likes Trevor, too. "At least he's useful," says my dad. The third member of Gramps' gang is Morris. Dad wouldn't describe Morris as useful. Morris is an entertainer, or at least he thinks he is. He's always cracking terrible jokes and doing impressions. He thinks he's a good singer, too. He used to work for British Rail before he retired. He made announcements at the station. He liked talking into a microphone so much he now does tours of local social clubs. He's worked out an act called 'Morris's

Microphone Mania'. Last month he got his first proper booking from the local cricket club. Dad was there. He said it was terrible. Morris said it just needed a bit of work. So now he's brushing it up and looking to do auditions for TV talent shows.

My gramps, Ken, wouldn't dream of going on TV – he's too shy. He spends a lot of time on his own in his potting shed. He loves growing things. He grows all sorts of things. He has a greenhouse and grows special plants that really should only grow in hot places. He grows plants for Winston. "Proper Caribbean plants," he calls them.

Next to the potting shed is Gramps'
pride and joy – his pigeon loft. Gramps
is a champion pigeon racer. He has
nine special racing pigeons and he
trains them every day. He's won prizes
and has loads of cups and trophies.
My dad says the pigeons are smelly
and noisy. He says Gramps talks to
them. He does too, because I think he
misses being at work. Gramps used to
be an accountant. He used to tell
people what to do. Now he talks to
plants and birds.

So Kenneth, Winston, Trevor and
Morris are Grandad's gang. Let me tell
you some of the things they get up to.

# Morris makes his mark

It was Friday night and Gramps and the gang were playing dominoes in the pub. Gramps had won the last four games in a row and Trevor was not happy. Winston wasn't very pleased either. He was beginning to fidget. When you can't complete your turn in dominoes you are supposed to tap the table to show that you can't go. It's called a 'knock'. Winston had knocked a lot and he was banging the table louder and louder each time that he couldn't go.

"Oi, keep the noise down over there," shouted Ted the landlord. "I've got other customers who've come out for a quiet drink. They don't want to be bothered by you lot."

"It's just me Caribbean ways," Winston replied. "We play the game with spirit in Tobago. Live life with spirit, it's the Caribbean way." Ted gave Winston a long, hard stare. "Well, if you want to take your mates over to Tobago and play dominoes outside in the sun, you can make as much noise as you like. I'll even come and serve you drinks, but in the meantime, here in my pub, keep the noise down." Everyone could see that Ted was serious and the gang carried on playing, but holding the dominoes like they were delicate china tea cups. Winston even stuck his little finger out like he was drinking tea when he laid his next domino. The game ended with another win for Gramps. He picked up 27p from the table.

"You're having a good run tonight, Ken." said Trevor. "Carry on like this and you'll be making more money than Morris makes from his entertaining." Everyone smiled. Word had got round about how bad Morris's entertainment had been at the cricket club. I suspect Dad had a fair bit to do with it. He hadn't stopped talking about it for days.

The gang started to make fun of

Morris.

"I hear your Cricket club do was as funny as a gorilla in the fridge," said Trevor. "Better than a bent banana," said Winston."

"Your magic was so good you made the audience disappear in ten seconds," said Ken. Everyone laughed again.

"OK, ok, so it didn't go so well" said Morris.

For once he went quiet and he seemed a bit hurt.

There was an awkward silence.

"Perhaps we could help," said Ken.

"It could be your material," said Trevor. "What did you give them?"

"Well, said Morris brightening. " I started with a round of jokes, did two brilliant magic tricks and ended with my big song *Please release me let me go.*

"Uhm," said Winston. "That song is a bit morbid. Couldn't you sing a happy one instead, or play a musical instrument.

"Well I did play trombone a bit in the railway workers band," said Morris. "But I don't have an instrument any more. I suppose I could try and borrow one from old......"

"No, no. You don't need to do that!" shouted Gramps suddenly. "You could make your own. You could play your own homemade musical instrument. You could give it a special name. You could make it look fantastic and it would be the only musical instrument like it in the world. It will be your unique selling point– Marvellous Morris and his whatever-you-call-it musical instrument!"

"Brilliant," said Trevor. "We can help you build it."

The gang stopped playing dominoes and started making suggestions about what Morris could do. Everyone chipped in.

Winston took a pencil from his pocket. "What you need to do is model it on a trombone- because you can play one

already. Then, in theory, you need to work out the harmonic series. It's quite simple it's, basic physics. It starts with an eight feet length of tubing."
Winston started drawing on a beer mat.

The gang set to work. The dominoes were put aside and the ideas for Morris's musical instrument took shape. Winston was in charge of the harmonic theory, Gramps chipped in about what it must look like, Morris kept referring to entertainment value and Trevor made a list of the materials and tools needed to build it. He made a long list including watering can, funnel and hose pipe. At midnight the plans were finished and the gang had one last beer before going home. They agreed that they would all meet up on Sunday afternoon at Trevor's house to start building.

Sunday afternoon arrived. There was much banging, shouting and tea-drinking in Trevor's shed. At 10 o'clock in the evening silence descended.

The gang stood around Morris's musical instrument feeling proud and happy. "What shall we call it?" asked Gramps. "It's got to have name, a unique name, one that will attract attention." After some discussion it was eventually agreed that it would be called *The Morrisophone.*

"Now all you've got to do is learn to play it," said Winston.

"No problem," said Morris. "I am a born entertainer. The show will go on." The next few days were quiet in Gramps' part of the village. But just up the road from our house it was a different matter. We live quite close to Morris in what Dad calls the 'cheap end of the village.' We could hear Morris in his garage blowing his Morrisophone. He was practising five hours a day. Dad said he would write to the council if it carried on. He was just about to go round and complain when Gramps arrived. "It's ok, I think he's perfected it now," said Gramps.

COME & BE ENTERTAINED BY...

# MARVELLOUS MORRIS
### AND HIS
# MORRISOPHONE

6.30PM THURSDAY AT

# THE RAILWAY SOCIAL CLUB

A WONDERFUL EVENT FOR ALL THE FAMILY

ADULTS £2 CHILDREN 50p

"Morris says he's ready for the first performance of his new show and you are all invited. Six thirty next Thursday at The Railway social club." Gramps handed me a fancy advertising leaflet that he had designed.

"I'd rather sit on an upside down hair brush," said Dad, but Mum and I worked on him and we all turned up with the rest of the gang for the wonderful event.

The club was quite full because a lot of people had come to hear a local man showing a film about his trip of a life time on an Indian mountain railway. He showed everyone a selection of special Indian tea bushes and fruits and he put them all on a table for people to look at. When he finished, Morris entered the stage. He began by introducing himself. "Welcome, I am Marvellous Morris and I'm here to entertain you." Then he told some jokes. "Ladies and gentlemen, what do you call two small cats that sit on your hands?...kerr.. mittens." Some people groaned but Morris pressed on. "Why did the cow cross the road?... to go to the mooovies." People groaned again. Somebody shouted 'get off' but Morris pressed on. He told some more bad jokes before he went onto his magic tricks and one of them was nearly quite good. He made an egg appear from a man's ear but Morris spoiled it by dropping the egg on the floor and slimy egg yolk splattered everywhere. Trevor rushed to wipe it up. "Get on to your musical instrument," he whispered. Morris did one more guess the card magic trick before he announced that he was reaching the climax of his show. He said he was about to perform something that no one in the world had ever performed before. "Ladies, gentlemen and children I will finish my entertainment by making music form ...not just..." and he reached into a bag, "a funnel, or just a hose pipe or even a watering can. I will make music from all of them together" and he fixed all of the parts together. "Ladies gentlemen and children, I give you The Morrisophone."

Morris then put his mouth to the pipe and blew. Phhhhrrr... furr....pooop... nothing happened. Morris looked at his Morrisophone. Something was wrong he couldn't make it work. People in the audience started booing. "Get off', "boo, boo!" was coming from all around the hall.

Morris was beginning to panic he
started to go red and someone shouted.
"The fruit on that table is funnier than
you." Morris looked at the fruit left by
the man before him. In his panic he
picked up an orange and shouted at

the audience. "Ladies and gentlemen my final ingredient for my Morrisophone is- an orange. I will now play for you." Morris put the orange into the funnel and everything worked. He played *She'll be coming round the mountain*. Morris danced about the stage as he played.

The audience were amazed. Trevor was singing along, gramps was jigging in his chair and Winston was break-dancing at the back of the hall. Even dad was smiling and singing the bits he knew.  When Morris finished, everyone clapped loudly. Trevor whistled through his fingers and some people shouted more! More!

Morris was smiling broadly. He bowed three times and left the stage with the applause still going on. Eventually he had to do an extra tune and he played *If you're happy and you know it,* as the audience sang along with him.

The evening had been a great success. Gramps, Winston and Trevor greeted Morris at the bar afterwards and shook his hand several times.

Marvellous Morris was an entertainer. Morris had made his breakthrough.

# Trevor builds his bridges

It was late in the afternoon and Trevor was on his way to our local primary school. Trevor was nervous. When he was a lad he never really liked school. He struggled with a lot of the work and didn't learn to read well until he was much older. Still, today was different Trevor was going to school as a guest. He had been invited to a meeting by the headteacher and the Chair of Governors. The school was about to celebrate its one hundred and fiftieth birthday and lots of special events were being planned. The school had invited all of its past pupils to a meeting to see if they would like to be involved in the celebrations. Trevor didn't really want to go but he knew the rest of the gang would be there and he didn't want to let the side down. Dad had been invited too.

The main door into the school was in the same place as it had always been but now it had a big glass porch before you got to it. Trevor had to press a button, talk into a little box, wait for a buzzing sound, sign in a big blue book, put his name on a badge then wait until he was buzzed in through another door. "Crikey it's like getting into a high security prison," muttered Trevor. "If I'd had to do this in my day I would never have gone to school."

Once inside Trevor was warmly greeted by Mrs Samson the headteacher. She shook Trevor's hand, offered him a cup of tea and smiled a lot. Trevor could see lots of other people sitting in rows and he saw the rest of the gang had kept a chair for him next to Winston. He was glad to sit down and be part of the crowd.

"Welcome everyone," said Mrs Samson. "I'm very pleased and proud to welcome you all to St Mary's school. I know that you have all been here before when you were just a little younger. This afternoon we want to share with you our plans for the school's one hundred and fiftieth birthday celebrations and we want to invite you all to join in." Mrs Samson carried on for another five minutes talking about continuity and heritage, and valuing the past to move on to the future before she announced that she would hand over to the school's Chair of Governors, Mrs Emily Trinity Fitzwarren.

A neat, slender woman stood up and began to talk. As soon as she did all of the gang looked at each other. Gramps had a strange smile on his face, and Morris moved his eyebrows up and down while nodding at the speaker. Winston whispered to Trevor, "Lord

preserve us, that's old Emily Toffee Socks. I didn't know she's the Chair of Governors."

"I didn't know she was still alive," whispered Trevor. "I haven't seen her for donkey's years."

Dad told me later that Gramps and the gang all went to primary school with Emily Trinity Fitzwarren, when she was still plain Emily Jones, before she got married. She left the school when she was nine years old to go to a posh private school and her family moved out of the village shortly afterwards. Dad said that she had married a famous banker and she now lived in the manor house in the next village.

That didn't interest me but I did want to know why she was called 'Toffee Socks'. Gramps explained that bit. He said that she was always playing tricks on the boys. She would pinch you then scream and tell the teachers that you had pinched her. She scribbled in Morris's books and he got told off for being messy and she once hid Winston's P.E. shorts and he had to do P.E. in his underpants. "The trouble was," said Gramps, "the teachers never believed us because she looked so innocent. Her hair was always in plaits, she was so neat and tidy and she always smiled sweetly at the teachers. In those days we used to have special 'sweet rewards Friday' assemblies and she got lots of sweets, usually toffees. She'd always take the sweet, smile and tuck it into the top of her sock. We decided to call her 'Toffee Socks Emily'. One day though, she went too far with Trevor and he got into big trouble. Trevor had spent weeks making a brilliant toy boat in Woodwork and when it was finished he was allowed to take it to the school pond at playtime and sail it. It went round in circles a bit and Emily was watching. When it sailed close to the edge she grabbed it and said it needed adjusting. She pulled the sail off and broke the mast. Trevor completely lost it. He grabbed her by her hair and dragged her to the outside playground water tap. He held her head under the tap and turned it on. She was soaked through.

There was an almighty fuss. Emily's mum came to the school and Trevor got the cane. He's never forgiven her."

At the end of the meeting in the school hall it was decided that everyone would celebrate the school's birthday by creating a brand new Birthday Garden. Mrs Samson explained that the children would design it and all of the adults could help with their own special skills. Gramps immediately volunteered to help with the growing of the plants. Winston said he would teach the children the science behind good plant cultivation and Morris said he would compose a special celebration song. Trevor didn't know what to do. He felt embarrassed and Mrs Samson noticed. She went over and spoke to him.

"Mrs Fitzwarren has been telling me she remembers you from her school days. She says you were a very practical person. We need people like you to help us make the children's ideas work. They always come up with brilliant ideas but can't always make them work. Would you be our practical construction advisor, Trevor?"

Trevor said yes and it was agreed that the children would write a letter to Trevor telling him about their ideas for building things in the garden. He would help them construct things.

A week went by and Trevor received a letter from the school. The children had all decided that their celebration garden should include a pond with water features. They wanted a small water slide that would turn a water wheel and best of all they wanted an island in the pond with a bridge to cross over to the island. A boy called Jack Simpson had designed the bridge. It was curved with wooden slats and metal handrails. Jack wanted lights on the wooden slats that lit up when you walked on them and best of all he wanted the bridge to swing into place when it was needed. He enclosed a diagram showing the bridge 'at rest' at the side of the pond and 'in place' connected to the island with lights flashing.

"I like this kid," Trevor said to himself. "I'll definitely help him make this." Jack and Trevor exchanged several more letters about the bridge and Trevor sorted out the materials and began construction. Emily Trinity Fitzwarren had persuaded her husband's bank to pay for it so Trevor could buy really good materials to build the bridge. He bought fancy, touch-sensitive lights and African hardwood for the slats. He and Jack decided that the bridge should have an electric motor so that the bridge could move in and out of position with a remote control. Trevor worked on the bridge every day for five weeks. When it was finished he invited the gang round to see it. Dad went too. They were all very pleased with it and took turns with the remote control, swinging the bridge from one position to another. Morris kept walking up and down it so that he could see the lights go on and off as he walked. They all agreed it was very good. Dad even said it was fantastic.

The work on the school garden was nearly finished and plans were made for the grand opening on the date of the school's one hundred and fiftieth birthday. Gramps and the gang helped to get the bridge to the school and put it in place. Mrs Samson said she had never seen such a beautiful bridge.

"Jack will be very proud. You should be too, Trevor." she said. Trevor went red and looked at his shoes.

Celebration Day arrived. The whole village was invited to the grand opening of the Birthday Garden. Hundreds of people turned up and everyone who helped with the garden was given three cheers by the children. Morris beamed as the children sang his song, and Gramps and Winston agreed that all of the plants looked in fine condition.

"I now call on our Chair of Governors, Mrs Emily Trinity Fitzwarren to cut the ribbon to officially open our garden," announced Mrs Samson. She handed a big pair of scissors to Mrs Fitzwarren. She waited while Jack Simpson pressed the remote control that swung the bridge into place. When the bridge was in position, Mrs Fitzwarren cut the ribbon at the entrance and took hold of Jack's hand. Together they walked across the bridge and the lights came on as they walked. When they got to the island they waved back to the crowd together and everyone cheered. The local newspaper took lots of pictures. Jack had handed the remote control to Trevor before he crossed. At the end of all of the cheering and photographs Jack ran back across the bridge. Trevor winked at him. Emily Trinity Fitzwarren began to make her way back across the bridge. She was still busy waving and smiling at all the cameras. She was half way over the bridge and not looking down so she didn't notice the bridge begin to move. It swung away from the bank and was half way out in the water. Emily Trinity Fitzwarren continued walking and smiling until SPLASH! Water flew through the air and her hat floated to the side while she stood knee deep in the middle.

"Oh dear, oh dear, what wonderful fun, how terribly refreshing," she said holding a fixed steely smile that

Gramps and the gang had all seen
before. "I've never had such fun." And
she splooshed, sploshed and waded her
way to the side.

Trevor handed the remote to Mrs
Samson and rushed to help the Chair
of Governors out of the pond. He held
out his hand to pull Emily
Trinity Fitzwarren out of the

celebration pond. He spoke quietly into her ear.

"Out you come, Toffee Socks," he said. "I think it needs adjusting."

Trevor had built his bridges.

# Winston fires the shots

It was a quiet Friday night game of Dominoes. No one in the gang was winning all of the games and everyone seemed happy just to be playing. The pub was quiet, too. Some of the louder, noisier regulars were away playing a darts match at The Rose and Crown. "It's a bit like a library in here tonight," said Trevor. "If this carries on we might have to talk to each other as well as play dominoes." Winston just smiled and nodded but he woke everyone up by knocking loudly on the table.

"Well I suppose we could tell each

other what we've been up to all week,"
said Gramps. "I've had quite a lot of
trouble with the greenfly. They're all
over the roses. I spent most of
yesterday spraying and trimming."

"You do lead an exciting life don't
you," said Morris sarcastically. "Roses,
plants, pigeons – you're like one of
those Hollywood superstars. It's all
action with you."

"OK, Mr Entertainment… what have
you been up to? I suppose you have
just signed a new contract for a tour of
Las Vegas."

"As it happens I have been busy
planning my next tour," said Morris. "I
was thinking of organising a tour of

Devon. I haven't been down that way for years now. It's a lovely part of the world. I thought I could do a four night tour of shows in some Devon clubs and see a bit of the countryside during the day. I tell you what, I could find a nice hotel and you could all come with me. We could call it a working holiday."

There was an awkward silence.

"Can't make it I'm afraid," said Trevor. "The under 12s football training is in full swing. Can't get away."

"Me neither," said Gramps. "I've got the East Anglia Pigeon Run to think about."

"I'm rather busy at work unfortunately," said Winston. "There's bit of a push on the *Vega* project. I've told them I'll work some extra days until it's all sorted."

There was another long silence and everyone just kept playing dominoes.

"So what's this Vega project then, Winston?" Trevor asked eventually.

"Oh, it's a job the lab has been working on for some time. The Vega company are very big in petrochemicals and now they want to break into the domestic cleaning market. They've got us working on a new washing detergent. They want to produce a washing powder that's brilliant at stain removal."

"Good grief," said Ken. "I get teased

about roses and pigeons and you spend your days with washing powder!"

Everyone laughed.

"Actually, it's more interesting than you might think," said Winston. "We've cracked the stain removing part of the equation. It's all basic science really. Enzymes combined with long molecule break up. No that's the easy bit. The hard part is not destroying the clothes when they get washed with the formula we've come up with. So far, we've created a washing powder that's really good at removing stains. The only problem is, after a couple of washes, it destroys the fabric of the clothes. Our first batch made great big holes in cotton shirts and it's even worse on wool. It practically destroyed a woollen jumper that we tried it on."

"You ought to give some to Morris," said Ken. "He could wash his clothes in your powder and then go on stage and do a whole new act – *Marvellous Morris and his disappearing clothes.*

Everyone thought this was very funny and other suggestions were made:

*For your eyes only – Morris's magic clothes.*

*The naked truth – Morris revealed* and *Bums away! A show that gets to the bottom of things.*

The last suggestion made the whole gang fall about laughing and they were still making a lot of noise when the darts team returned.

"Eh up! The grandads are in and they've been taking their happy pills," said Gary Sutcliffe. "It's nice to see you old boys have still got the energy to laugh," and he went straight to the bar. "Four of our specials please Ted. We the Jolly Farmer's darts team have won again. Top of the league. Time to celebrate with our secret weapon – Manchester's finest ale *Didsbury Deadbeat*, wonderful stuff. You old boys ought to try it. It might help you enjoy yourselves a bit more often. It's ten times better than that local stuff you lot drink."

Gary Sutcliff didn't grow up in our village. Dad says he moved in from Manchester ten years ago. Dad says he's alright but he's a bit loud. He's always going on about how rubbish things are in our village and how everything is better in Manchester. He's persuaded Ted to sell his favourite beer *Didsbury Deadbeat* and he bullies the other member of the darts team into drinking it as well. They only drink it when they're with him. Dad says they really prefer the local beer.

Now, Winston's a quiet man most of the time, but he doesn't particularly like Gary. My dad says Gary rubs him up the wrong way. Winston likes the local ale and he was not prepared to let Gary get away with his last remark.

"You say it's better Gary but that's because you've got no taste," Winston replied. "You call it ale and it isn't. There are no hops in it. It is not made with barley and the yeast content is far too high. I know, I've done a chemical analysis of it in the lab. It's basically coloured water with synthetic flavourings and added fizz. It's a mass-produced chemical product. I wouldn't even call it beer."

"Oh you wouldn't, would you Winston?" Gary replied and he moved over to the domino table close to Winston.

"I suppose you would know all about that what with your university degree and your Caribbean ways. You know what, Winston? You have spent so many years drinking that local stuff it's addled your brain."

Winston made a move to get up from the table. Gramps could see things were getting tense.

"Why don't you tell us one of your latest jokes Morris," said Gramps. "Tell us the one about the parrot and the sports car," and he winked at Morris. Morris caught his eye and went on to tell a long joke that was so bad that everyone just moaned at the end. Gary walked back to his mates at the bar.

"Why do you let him wind you up?" Trevor asked Winston. "He's just full of hot air. He's always been like it."

"Well his hot air is based on ignorance and I can't stand ignorance," said Winston and the gang went back to playing dominoes. Gary and the darts team told Ted how brilliant they had been at darts at the Rose and Crown. Winston spent the next ten minutes telling the gang about the scientific principles of making real ale.

"He's such a loud mouth I'd like to put him in his place," said Winston.

"Well you won't get him onto university challenge will you?" said Trevor and everyone chuckled. It was then that Ted came over to them.

"Now then lads," he said. "Are you lot up for my latest Jolly Farmer outing? I've organised a pub day out and I need one more team of four to take the last place. We're going to one of those paint ball evenings out at Fenton woods. You get to run about the woods, shoot paint pellets at each other and have a bit of fun. We need six teams of four. We all go out into the woods with the paint guns and try to shoot paint at each other. Each team has a different colour and the winner is the team that gets most of their colour onto the other teams. You lose a point for each paint mark you get on your team. So the idea is to shoot well but avoid getting shot yourselves. At the end of the evening we all come back here and the winning team gets four free pints of their favourite beer. Are you up for it?"

"Oh, I don't know," said Morris.

"Seems a bit messy to me."

"I'm not sure about crawling around in woodland. We're not as young as we used to be," said Gramps.

"We could do some training first," said Trevor.

"Well have a think about it," said Ted. "Five pounds each for a fun event. Remember it's the last team place left. The darts team have just signed up."

Gary was listening to Ted.

"Don't bother with them Ted, they're too old. Zimmer frames are no good in the woods. Leave it to us boys. We'll beat the rest of them for you. You can join us later and watch us drink our free *Didsbury Deadbeat.* Cheers!" and Gary raised his glass towards Winston.

"Count us in Ted," said Winston and he handed a twenty pound note to Ted.

"What have you done?" whispered Morris.

"Don't worry boys," said Winston. "Gary's loud but all he has is ignorance.

I have knowledge."

Gramps and the gang were not pleased with Winston. They were not sure about paint ball but Winston seemed determined and he persuaded them to meet him to talk about it at his house the next day. He said he had a plan. The gang met at Winston's. "Basically," he said. "This paint ball competition is about the application of science."

"No its not," said Morris. "It's about getting messy and hiding behind trees."

"And shooting guns. I'm hopeless at that sort of thing," said Gramps.

"We can learn that bit," said Trevor. "You used to be a good shot at the fairground gun range."

"That was a long time ago," said Gramps.

"Don't worry," said Winston. "We've got it covered. Trevor has got hold of four of those high powered water pistols and he's adapted them to take little water pellets that he's made out of cling film. He'll train you how to shoot. All you've got to do is practise. I have the one thing that will guarantee we win," and Winston showed them a large tin with powder in it.

"Gentleman, he said, I give you the very first *Vega One* prototype we produced at the lab. This stuff removes paint stains in ten minutes. It doesn't matter how many times we get shot in the competition all we've got to do is remove the paint stains before the final count up."

"But what about the holes?" asked Morris. "You said it made holes in the clothes."

"Oh it does," said Winston. "But the overalls they give you at the paint ball place are made out of synthetic nylon. The holes don't appear on synthetics for forty-eight hours. I know, I tested it. We will be gone and enjoying our prizes before anyone notices."

"Brilliant," said Gramps. "I think I might enjoy this after all."

The paint ball competition was two weeks away and Gramps and the gang spent a lot of time at Trevor's practising shooting. He showed them how to shoot lying down, standing up and kneeling down. Trevor, Winston, Ken and Morris soon became hotshots.

The day of the paint ball competition arrived. Gramps and his gang walked to the car park of the Jolly Farmer

where a coach was waiting to take
everyone to Fenton woods. The darts
team were already there and on the
coach along with two other teams; Ted
the landlord's team and the crib team.
"Just the quiz team and the Hooper
family to come," said Ted.
When everyone was finally on board
the coach they headed out of the
village. They travelled along a
motorway for a short while before
turning onto smaller roads, up some
hills and into the woods.
"Have you all got your *Vega One?*"
whispered Morris to the gang.
"Remember, keep it hidden and try not
to lose it." Gramps had told everyone

to put the powder in small plastic bags and tape them to their ankles under their socks. Everyone checked their ankles and nodded.

The coach pulled into Fenton woods and a man dressed like a soldier welcomed them off the coach.

"Welcome to Fenton Events. You are all going to enjoy a stimulating adventure this evening. My name is Bob and it is my job to make sure you enjoy yourselves and stay safe. The first thing to do is change into your fighting colours. Each team will have a different colour fighting suit and that will be the same colour as the paint balls in your guns. Listen to your colours then go into the changing rooms and get changed. Bob called out the teams' colours – green, yellow, purple, blue, grey and black.

"Hey Bob, would you mind if my team had red? It's my lucky colour," shouted Gary.

"Well sir, I can give you red if you like, but if you wear red suits up here in the woods everyone will see you clearly and you will be an easy target."

Gary looked embarrassed and said he would stick with blue. Gramps' team were given grey suits and were told that their guns actually fired white paint so that it could be seen easier for scoring.

When everyone had changed, Bob took all the teams deep into the woods and made them stand on a concrete circle. "This is the start and finish base," said Bob. "Now remember, every one of you has twenty-five pellets in your gun, so your maximum number of team hits is one hundred. At the end of the shoot we count up the number of paint splats on each person. The team with the highest number of hits wins. Try to shoot straight and not be seen yourself."

Bob then gave each team a map of the shooting area in the wood. It had places to hide and things to climb up on, walls, ditches, streams, old buildings, even an old quarry with rock boulders and a cave.

"Right, you have five minutes to study the map then set off into the woods. You cannot begin shooting until you hear me sound the siren. Put your safety helmets and visors on. Off you go!"

Winston told the gang that the best plan was to split up. "We don't need to move about too much. Find somewhere to hide where you can see other people moving, and then pick them off as they move."

Gramps got himself behind a large rock in the quarry. He heard the siren sound and noticed two of the yellow team still in the open. He fired two quick shots.

Two hits straight away.

"Yes!" whispered Gramps. "This is going to be fun."

Morris decided to go into some thick grass. He lay on his tummy behind a bush.

Trevor positioned himself behind the wall of an old building. Winston took himself to a collection of wooden poles and a platform quite near to Gramps. As he got into place he felt a flick on his stomach and he looked down to see blue paint. "Got you!" shouted Gary, and he fired three more shots at Winston. "Look out!" shouted Gramps. Gary heard him, turned round and

fired two more paint balls at Gramps.
"Blimey he's fast," muttered Gramps.

Gary ran around the shooting area like
a maniac. The rest of his team were
running around the woods, too.

Morris's place in the long grass was a good choice as he shot off fifteen pellets in ten minutes. After half an hour Trevor was sure that he had made fourteen hits and Gramps thought he had scored twelve. Winston checked his gun and his watch. Fifteen minutes left and six more pellets. He looked at his shooting suit – it was covered in paint splodges. Time for the *Vega One,* thought Winston. He pulled the powder from his sock and started rubbing at the paint. "Blue ones first," he said to himself. The paint began to vanish. "Brilliant stuff this!" grinned Winston.

At the same time the other members of

the gang began rubbing away with the *Vega One*. Trevor cleaned away five paint spots. Gramps had managed to make six paint marks disappear and was just starting on the seventh spot when he heard a loud cry of pain. This was followed by shouting and lots of shooting of guns. He also heard Gary's voice laughing. Morris was shouting "that's not fair, that's not fair!"

The siren went. It was the end of the game. Everyone trudged back to the concrete circle. Morris came out of the grass. He was covered in paint marks. "I fell into some stinging nettles – it really hurt and I couldn't help shouting out. Some of the other teams heard me and fired all their remaining shots at me. It was terrible. Sorry lads."

"Don't be sorry, use your *Vega One* quickly," said Winston and Morris started to rub at the paint.

By the time everyone had got back to the concrete circle Morris had got rid of some of the paint but he was still very colourful. Winston looked closely at everyone. He knew the final score was going to be close. Winston is brilliant at maths and he had worked out the final score in his head before Bob arrived.

"Just one more," he said to himself and he stretched into his sock. He hid the powder in his hand and walked over to

Morris. "Stand still," he whispered and patted Morris on the back with the hand that held the *Vega One*.

"Bad luck old boy," he said as he rubbed away at a blue spot on Morris's back with the *Vega One*. The spot disappeared.

Bob went around everyone with a notepad and pencil and counted all the different coloured paint hits. When he had added them all up, he announced the results.

"I hope you have all enjoyed your time at Fenton woods. We have some high scores this evening." Gary gave a big cheesy grin to Winston.

"In last place with a score of 42 points,

it's Ted the Landlord's team. Fifth place with 46 is the quiz team. Fourth place with 47 points –the Hooper family. Third place with 52 points is the crib team. So the winner tonight is between Gary's darts team and Winston's domino team. The runners up with a very good score of 63 are... the darts team! The dominoes team take it by one point with 64."

Gary stalked off into the changing rooms.

Back at the Jolly Farmer, Gramps' gang celebrated with their free pint of local beer. Gary was very quiet as he sucked his *Didsbury Deadbeat* out of the bottle.

"Well," said Ted. "I didn't expect this. I didn't think you old boys would do so well. How did you do it?"

"Knowledge," said Winston.

# Kenneth flies like a bird

Ken was waiting outside the local newsagents. He had bought his normal newspaper and was standing next to the village notice board. He looked at it carefully. Plenty of notices about parish council meetings, playgroups and scouts but not the notice he was looking for. He looked at his watch. 8 a.m. Monday 17$^{th}$ – it should be on display by now. He was just about to go back into the shop to complain when he saw the vicar striding towards him.

"Bang on time as usual Ken," said the vicar.

"Actually, I was just wondering what had happened to you," Ken replied. "I make it five past eight."

"Good things come to those who wait," said the vicar and he undid the parish notice board cover and pinned a notice onto the board.

"I know this is what you're waiting for," he said and he stood back so that Ken could read it.

# Annual St. Mary's Sunflower Challenge

Once again I am pleased to announce the official opening of the St. Mary's Sunflower Challenge: our annual competition to find the special sunflower.

This year, as usual, there will be four different clues. The first clue is posted below. The next three will follow each Monday on this notice board.

Winner announcement and prize-giving will take place at the village barn dance on Saturday 20$^{th}$.

To take part please register with Mr Patel at the newsagents.

The prize this year has generously been donated by Fenton Events Ltd.

*A woodland Jeep Safari for four people*

Entrance fee £5 per adult. Children's sunflower-growing completion 50p

**Clue number one:**
**Follow the path to eastern promise.**

Good luck and remember to spread a little sunshine.

D. Cutler
Vicar St. Mary's

Ken finished reading the notice and carefully wrote down the clue on the back of an old envelope.

"Is that it Vicar? Follow the path to eastern promise. That's not much. You usually give a lot more in your first clue."

"Not this year Ken," said the vicar. "I have tried to be a bit more cryptic. I don't want to get stuck in a rut. I think one or two people have worked out my clue-setting style. It's good to have a change. Anyway, I am sure you will manage. You're one of our regulars. I don't think you've ever missed a year have you Ken?"

"No," said Ken. "Every year for seven

years. Second place four times, third twice and unplaced only one. I'm going to win it this year, Vicar. Hope springs eternal! –That's what they say isn't it?"

"They do indeed Ken. Good luck."

The vicar walked away as briskly as he had arrived. Ken looked again at the notice and pondered the clue. He kept repeating it in his head as he walked home.

Now, my dad says the annual sunflower challenge is really difficult. He and mum enter every year as do lots of other people in our village. It's become really popular since the vicar first introduced it when he came to the village. The vicar has a bit of a thing about sunflowers. He says they are happy plants, and the world needs plenty of happiness, so he introduced the sunflower challenge. Basically it's a sort of treasure hunt but instead of hunting treasure you have to find a special sunflower. Every year the vicar grows a sunflower from seed and when it's about 30 cm tall he sneaks off from the vicarage and plants it somewhere secret. It's always planted within a five kilometre radius of the church and the vicar goes to a lot of trouble to plant it somewhere really difficult to find. Last year he planted it in an old scrap yard. The year before that, he planted it in the middle of a field of corn. He's even planted it in the graveyard near the church but it's always difficult to find. The thing is, the sunflower grows very quickly so it should get easier to find as the days and weeks go by. Each week for four weeks every Monday at 8 o'clock in the morning the vicar adds a new clue on the village notice board. To make sure no one cheats the vicar puts a special tag around the stalk of the sunflower. The winner is the person who finds the sunflower and collects the tag. If no one finds it everyone says where they think it is and the vicar gives the prize to the person who is closest.

Because Ken likes plants and gardening

so much he takes the competition really seriously. He says he knows about sunflowers and where they like to grow. The trouble is, there is one other person in the village who takes it seriously as well and he has won the competition for the last four years running. He is called Albert Betteridge. Ken does not like Albert – they are rivals at a lot of things. They both grow lots of plants, they're both good at gardening and Albert even says he's good at dominoes but he never plays with Gramps and his gang. Anyway, the fact that Albert has won the challenge for the last four years is really getting to Ken.

"I'm going to get him this year," Ken said to his racing pigeons as he was cleaning out their loft. "He thinks he's clever but this year I have got my secret weapon and it's all thanks to you boys."

Ken finished cleaning the pigeon loft and made sure the birds had enough grain and water, and then he walked up to his house to get ready for the gang. They were coming to help him with his master plan to win the sunflower challenge.

When all of the gang had arrived, Ken told them how much he wanted to win and how if they all worked together they would have a good chance.

"You may have got this winning thing a bit out of proportion Ken," said Winston.

"We know you're not keen on Albert," said Morris. "But why do you keep..."

"What do you want us to do?" Trevor interrupted. He could see Ken was becoming agitated. "We're here to help," said Trevor.

"Thanks Trev," said Ken. "Well it starts with the clues. If we put our heads together each Monday we can break the clues and then each of us can use our special talents to find the sunflower. Trevor, you take that Austin Seven of yours out for a run most days. You could be the lookout man. Change your route a bit, stay within the five kilometre radius and look out for the flower. Winston you're a scientist, you can help me analyse sunflower seeds and Morris, you're an entertainer. You're good at talking and kidding people so you can put Albert off the scent by spreading false rumours about the sunflower's whereabouts."

"I'm not sure I like..." Morris began.

"Be quiet and start to help," said Trevor.

"There's one more thing," said Ken. "This year I'm going to use Portland Porker."

"Portland Porker?" said Winston. That's one of your racing pigeons isn't it?"

"Exactly," said Ken. "Porker is going to help too."

My dad says Gramps' racing pigeons are really good. All of them have won races. All except Portland Porker. He was Gramps' first ever racing pigeon. Dad says Gramps treats him like a pet. Portland Porker sits on Gramps' shoulder. He makes special cooing noises when Gramps goes near the pigeon loft. Gramps talks to him all the time. He even has his own special nest box. Dad says Gramps called him Portland Porker because he eats so much. He's never won a race because he's more interested in eating than racing. Every time he sets off in a race he makes his way to the nearest source of food, fills his tummy then flies slowly back to Gramps' pigeon loft. He's always last but Gramps loves him. "How on earth is a racing pigeon going to help us win the challenge?" asked Winston.

"Easy," said Gramps. "I've been feeding Porker a special diet of sunflower seeds. He loves them. I've even added sunflower petals to his diet so he can help us find the vicar's sunflower. All we've got to do is take Porker out every day. That's where you come in Trevor. You can take him in your car. You just need to release him at the edge of the five kilometre radius and we wait for him to come home and see if he's eaten sunflowers."

"I suppose you'll just ask him to tell you were the sunflower is? Or will you get him to draw you a map?" said Morris.

"Don't be sarcastic Morris. The answer

will be in his poo. When Porker gets
back we just wait for him to poo, then
I give the poo to Winston and he takes

it to the lab to analyse. You can tell
what a bird has eaten by examining the
poo can't you Winston?"

"Well yes, in theory, but I've never
done it," said Winston.

"Don't worry," said Ken. I know the
gang can make this plan work."

Ken and the gang spent the rest of the
morning sorting out the final details of
the plan.

They started with a large map and
drew a five kilometre radius circle on it
with the church at the centre.

"Now the first clue," said Gramps.
"Follow the road to eastern promise."

"We've got to go east from the church.
I've not fed Porker today. Trev, you

take him out tomorrow and release him. He'll be starving and he'll go straight for his favourite food – sunflower seed."

Next day Trevor released Porker in the agreed spot five kilometers east of the church. Two hours later Porker arrived back at the pigeon loft. Gramps waited for him to poo then passed it on to Winston who took it to the lab. Two days later the results were in: Porker had eaten mostly cabbage and a few grains of corn. No sunflower. "We'll have to do it again," said Ken and Trevor took Porker to a slightly different place east of the church. Still no sunflower poo.

By now it was time for the second clue. Morris was given the job of going to collect it from the notice board. When he arrived Albert Betteridge was already there.

"Hello Morris," said Albert. How's it going? I hear you and Ken are working together this year."

"Well," said Morris. "I think we've nearly cracked it. I've heard a rumour that the vicar has done his graveyard trick again. I shouldn't be telling you this but we've found out one of the gravestones has an inscription on it that says 'eastern promise.' The trouble is we can't find it."

"Oh, can't you?" said Albert, and he

gave Morris a suspicious look. "Well maybe this second clue will help."
They both looked at clue number two on the notice board.

> Postmen always deliver
> to the King.

"Crikey, that's a strange one," said Morris and he took the clue to the rest of the gang.
"Postmen... it's got to be something to do with addresses."
"What about street names?" said Trevor.
"Look at the map. How many street names are named after kings of England?"

"Don't forget it's east of the church," said Gramps and they all stared at the map again.

"Here we go," said Morris. "Just two royal street names east of the church – George Street and King Edward Street, it's got to be close to one of those."

Trevor was dispatched to take Porker to King Edward Street and let him go. Meanwhile the rest of the gang drove out to George Street. They wandered around looking over walls and peering in hedges but they did not see any sunflowers. Next day Porker's bird poo results came back. No sunflowers eaten.

The gang continued to walk around

George Street and King Edward Street for the next two days but they found nothing.

Monday arrived with the third clue. Morris met Albert again and this time told him a story about a postman who used to live in the village. He told Albert that he was buried in the churchyard. Albert pretended not to be interested.

"Well," Albert said, "I don't think clue three has anything to do with the churchyard."

> A hungry man needs a bold heart.
> A well-fed man chops sticks
> for the fire.

"What an earth is that about?" asked Morris.

"No idea," said Albert, but Morris thought he saw a sneaky smile.

Back at Ken's house the gang were trying to work out clue three.

"Good grief, this clue seems to be about food not kings," said Winston.

"Well I'm still sure the postman clue is about a street name," said Trevor.

"Perhaps we should look for street names of kings inside the whole of the five kilometre radius not just east of the church."

"Good idea," said Morris and he went onto the internet and came back with a list of all the street names around the village. "The only royal ones are George and Edward and we've got those already," he said.

Ken looked down the list.

"Yes," he said. "But we haven't looked at this one. Look! Lionheart Crescent, out near Dalton. King Richard was called Lion heart. He was a king."

"But it's not in the east," said Trevor.

"Lionheart Crescent is south west from the church and it's full of shops and take-aways."

"Exactly," said Ken. "And one of those take-aways is Chinese. Chinese food is eastern food."

"And the Chinese take-away in Lionheart Crescent is called 'Dragon fire' and they serve food with chop sticks," said Morris.

All the members of the gang looked at each other. They had connected all of the clues. They knew they were on to something.

"That's it!" said Ken. "It's Lionheart Crescent. Let's get down there – we can release Porker as well. We can see what he comes up with."

Porker was let out to fly at the edge of the five mile radius in line with Lionheart Crescent. Afterwards his poo was analysed. Winston phoned the results to Ken. "We've got a positive," he said. "Porker has eaten sunflower."

"Good old Porker," said Ken and he

went down to the pigeon loft to talk to Porker. Portland Porker cooed into Ken's ear.

The next few days were very busy. The gang spent a lot of time around Lionheart Crescent. They looked in every place they thought a sunflower would grow. On their third day in the crescent Morris saw Albert Betteridge.

"You and your mates look busy," he said. "Do you know something I don't?" he said before grinning and driving away in his car.

"I think he's got it," said Trevor.

"I'm not sure," said Ken and he let Porker fly away one more time.

The next day was Monday, the day of

the final clue. Morris went to the notice board. His heart sank like a stone.

---

**St Mary's Sunflower challenge**
No clue four needed
The sunflower has been found.
The winner will be announced next
Saturday at the barn dance.

---

When Morris told the gang they all went very quiet. They all agreed they would go to the barn dance to find out who had won the prize even though they didn't want to see Albert Betteridge looking smug.

"I was hoping we could all go on a Jeep woodland safari," said Trevor.

"Perhaps we'll go another time," said

Ken, and he went to the pigeon loft to talk to Porker.

Saturday arrived and the gang went to the barn dance. Dad was busy making a fool of himself dancing and the gang joined in the dances they knew. During the interval the vicar climbed onto the stage.

"Ladies and gentlemen, it is my pleasure to announce the winner of the eighth St Mary's Sunflower Challenge. Will the winner please come onto the stage?" Albert Betteridge walked on to the stage.

"Vicar," he said. "I have here a photograph of me with the sunflower in the delivery yard of the Dragon Fire

Chinese restaurant. That's where you hid the sunflower."

"Indeed I did," said the vicar. "But do you have the special tag to show that you got there first?" Albert looked a little bothered.

"Well vicar, I think this year you must have forgotten to put it on. I couldn't find it but I found the sunflower."

"I didn't forget it, Albert. You found the sunflower but not the tag because you got to the flower second. You are this year's runner up. Please will the real winner of the sunflower challenge come onto the stage?" Everyone looked around. Albert looked very puzzled. After a dramatic silence Ken held up his hand.

"Here I am vicar. I've got the tag. I found the flower last Friday and Mr Yang took a picture of me removing the tag in his delivery yard." Ken showed everyone a large photograph and everyone started clapping.

"Go Ken, go!" shouted the gang.

The vicar presented Ken with his prize.

"I'm going to take my mates on a woodland jeep safari," he said. The gang cheered.

Next Friday in the Jolly Farmer, Winston was laying out the dominoes on the table.

"I know you wanted to keep your win a secret to give us a surprise," said Winston. "But you never told us how you actually found the sunflower."

"Well," said Ken. "I let Portland Porker go one more time, early in the morning and this time I followed him. He took me straight to it.

You guys are brilliant and I can talk to pigeons."

That's Grandad's gang.

# Adrian Townsend

Lives in Oxford. He likes playing golf, football and dominoes as well as writing stories.

He can be contacted on E mail at

Hidip@aol.com

If you enjoyed this book, look out for
other stories by the same author
including

**Naughty Lessons**
**Gran's Gang**
**Gran's Gang Go To Spain**
**Gran's Gang Solve a**
**Mystery**
and
**Teachers' Tales**